Star Friends

SECRET SPELL

To Spike, who gives me so
many amazing ideas! – LC

To Katie – LF

STRIPES PUBLISHING
An imprint of the Little Tiger Group
1 Coda Studios, 189 Munster Road,
London SW6 6AW

A paperback original
First published in Great Britain in 2018

Text copyright © Linda Chapman, 2018
Illustrations copyright © Lucy Fleming, 2018

ISBN: 978-1-84715-905-2

Star Friends
Secret Spell

LINDA CHAPMAN
ILLUSTRATED BY LUCY FLEMING

IN THE STAR WORLD

A snowy owl, a badger, a stag and a wolf gathered by a waterfall of falling stars. Their fur and feathers glittered with stardust and their eyes were a deep indigo blue. The owl hooted softly. "My friends, let us see what is happening with the young animals and their Star Friends in the human world."

As he touched the surface of the pool with the tip of his wing, an image slowly formed. Four girls and four animals with indigo eyes were settling down for the night. A girl with dark-blond hair was hugging a fox, a girl with black curls was cuddling a red squirrel, a girl with long dark brown hair was stroking a deer and a girl with red hair was curled up beside a wildcat with a tabby coat.

"They all look happy," said the badger with a sigh of relief.

Hunter the owl nodded. "The young animals are doing well. They have been teaching their Star Friends how to use magic to keep the human world safe. The good deeds they have done so far have strengthened the magic current that flows between our world and the human world, and has made their magical abilities stronger."

The wolf stiffened. "The picture is changing!"

A new image formed, showing a person wearing a black hooded robe and holding a stone bowl filled with small objects. Shadows were swirling up from the ground.

The stag pawed the earth in alarm.
"Someone is working dark magic near the Star
Friends!"

The owl nodded gravely. "I'm afraid it
appears to be as we suspected. Two Shades
have already been defeated by the Star Animals
and their friends. But now more trouble is
coming their way."

The wolf growled. "I believe I know this

person we can see."

"You do, my friend," said the owl. "She has caused problems in the past. Her magic was once bound but now she is able to use it again."

"What can we do to stop her?" said the stag.

"Nothing." The owl shook his head. "It is up to the new Star Animals and their friends to stop this threat. All we can do is watch."

"And hope the dark magic does not win," said the wolf grimly.

CHAPTER ONE

Maia stood on a bridge. On one side, a dark mist rose from the ground. Maia's blood turned to ice as the mist took the shape of a tall thin figure. It was a Shade – an evil spirit from the shadows who liked to hurt and harm people.

As the Shade fixed its eyes on her, Maia looked around desperately. Where was Bracken, her Star Animal? And where were her friends and their Star Animals?

"Let me past!" the Shade hissed.

Maia stood her ground. "No!"

In a shimmer of starlight, a fox with indigo eyes appeared beside her.

"Bracken!" Maia whispered in relief.

Bracken leaped between Maia and the Shade. "Go back to the shadows!" he growled.

The Shade sniggered. "Why should we listen to you? Only a Spirit Speaker can command us."

Maia's heart missed a beat as more dark shapes started to form behind the first Shade.

They spoke with one eerie voice. "You may have defeated the Wish Shade but the one using dark magic has conjured more of us. She wants us to make all your fears come true!"

Stepping forwards, the first Shade swiped at Bracken, who yelped in pain as sharp nails scratched him.

"Bracken!" Maia screamed.

Maia felt something licking her nose.

"I'm here, Maia."

Hearing Bracken's voice, she blinked open
her eyes and looked into his anxious face.
Then she felt a hand on her shoulder and heard
Sita gently saying, "Maia, wake up!"

Maia's heart gradually slowed. She was in
her bedroom with Bracken on her lap and Sita
kneeling beside her. Sita's Star Animal, a gentle
deer called Willow, was next to Sita while
Lottie and Ionie were still fast asleep on the
floor nearby with their Star Animals – a red
squirrel and a wildcat. The grey light of dawn
was just streaking across the sky.

"Were you having a bad dream?" Sita
whispered.

Maia nodded. "It was about a Shade." She shivered as she remembered. "Lots of Shades. Bracken got hurt. It was horrible."

Bracken licked her hand and Maia wrapped her arms round him. She couldn't bear the thought of Bracken being injured. Ever since they had become Star Friends a few weeks ago, she had felt a deep bond with him – she loved him more than anything in the world.

It's like he's part of me, she realized.

The day she had met him in a clearing in the woods was etched into her mind. To Maia's amazement, he had talked to her, telling her he was from a different world and that if she wanted to be his Star Friend he would teach her how to use magic to do good and make the world a better place. Most importantly of all, they had to stop anyone who was trying to use dark magic to hurt others. It had been even more amazing when her best friends had become Star Friends, too.

"You probably had a nightmare because of that horrible Wish Shade we fought last night," Sita said. "But Ionie sent it back to the shadows, remember? It's gone. There's nothing to worry about."

As Maia felt her fear fade, she wondered if Sita was using her special magic abilities. The Star Animals had taught them all how to use the magic current that flowed between the human world and the Star World. The girls had found they each had different skills. Maia could see things that were happening elsewhere and look into the future; Sita could heal and soothe; Lottie was amazingly agile and Ionie could shadow-travel. Not only that, Ionie was also a Spirit Speaker, which meant she could command Shades and send them back to the shadows.

Maia gave Sita a grateful look. "You're right. I'm sorry I woke you up."

"Maia, what did you see?" Bracken asked.

"Does it matter?" Sita said. "It was just a dream."

Bracken looked anxious. "I'm not sure. As Maia's magic sight abilities get stronger, there might be things in her dreams that come true."

Maia felt a flicker of alarm and tried to remember. "I was on a bridge and the Shade said something about the one who had conjured the Wish Shade calling more Shades … and then lots more of them appeared. Then the Shade attacked."

"I hope it doesn't come true," said Sita. "It was scary enough facing just one Shade last night. I don't want to have to fight lots of them."

Just then Ionie sat up sleepily and pushed her red hair out of her face. "What's going on?"

Beside her Sorrel the wildcat stretched and rolled on to her back. "I refuse to believe it's morning yet," she yawned. "Whatever it is, it can wait."

"No, it can't. This could be important. Wakey-wakey, pussycat," said Bracken, jumping over Sorrel's tummy and landing on the end of her fluffy tail. "We all need to talk."

The wildcat leaped to her feet and hissed. But Bracken ignored her and trotted over to wake Juniper the squirrel and Lottie, who were curled up together inside Lottie's sleeping bag. Juniper squeaked in protest and snuggled closer into Lottie's arms so Bracken kept licking them both until they woke up.

Soon the girls were all sitting round in a circle, cuddling their animals.

"If Bracken's right and Maia's dream *is* true," said Ionie, "then we have to try and find out who is conjuring these Shades."

"The Shade said it was a woman," Maia remembered. "And that she's the same person who conjured the Wish Shade."

"I wish we could use your magic to find out more, Maia," said Lottie.

Maia wished that, too, but she had already tried to see who had conjured the Wish Shade and her magic had shown her nothing but darkness. Bracken had told her it seemed as though the person was using a spell to conceal herself.

"We should start by finding out who gave the little garden gnome with the Wish Shade trapped inside to Paige's family," said Ionie. "We need to know if that person knew about the Wish Shade and that it was going to make wishes come true in a horrible way."

Maia nodded. "I asked Paige once and she said

that the gnome was from a friend of her mum's. We need to find out her name." She jumped to her feet. "Let's go to Paige's house now."

Ionie leaped up, too. "Yes, let's!"

"Wait!" said Lottie. "Everyone will still be in bed."

"Oh yes," said Ionie, looking disappointed.

Maia sighed. Now they had a plan she wanted to act on it right away.

"While we're waiting you could all try doing some magic," Bracken said. "Maia's magic seems to have got stronger from defeating the Shade yesterday, so maybe everyone else's will have, too."

Juniper jumped on to Maia's desk, his tail curling behind him. "You might all be able to do new things!"

"Oh, I hope so! I can already do so many cool things with my magic, imagine if I could do even more," said Ionie.

Maia saw Lottie roll her eyes. Ionie

sometimes said things that made her sound boastful and it really irritated Lottie. It used to annoy Maia, too, but now Maia was beginning to think Ionie didn't mean to show off, she just didn't always think about how what she said would sound to other people.

"We could go to the clearing," said Willow.

Bracken yapped in agreement, Juniper chattered happily and Sorrel nodded her head. The animals all loved the clearing in the woods. It was where they had first appeared when they had travelled from the Star World and it was an especially magical place.

Juniper leaped on to Lottie's shoulder. "When we're at the clearing we might also find out which of you is the super-strong one the Wish Shade spoke about."

Maia felt a jolt run through her. Just before the Wish Shade had been sent back to the shadows, it had told them that one of them would turn out to be incredibly powerful – so powerful that the person using dark magic would be scared of them.

"I'd forgotten about that," said Sita.

"Me, too," said Lottie.

"It's obviously going to be Ionie," declared Sorrel. "She can shadow-travel and command Shades already."

Ionie looked pleased.

"It might not be Ionie," protested Lottie. "It could be Maia or Sita."

"Oh, I don't want it to be me," said Sita hurriedly. "I'm happy just healing people."

"It could be you, Lottie," Maia put in. "Your agility is incredible. I wish I could run and jump and climb like you."

Bracken put his paws up on Maia's leg. "I bet you're the special one, Maia," he whispered.

Maia hugged him. She really hoped so!

Sorrel trotted to the door, her tail ramrod straight. "Why are you all standing around talking?" she said. "Let's go!"

CHAPTER TWO

The girls pulled on their clothes. As they left Maia's bedroom the animals vanished – it was important for them to stay secret from other humans.

Ionie fell into step beside Maia as they went downstairs. "This is really exciting, isn't it?" she said in a low voice. "We might all have new powers. And it sounds like there will be more Shades for us to fight."

Maia nodded in agreement. Although Shades were scary, she felt a thrill at the thought of using her magic to stop them. "Last night was exciting, wasn't it?" she said to Ionie.

Ionie grinned. "Stalking a possessed gnome, rescuing friends from a burning shed and using magic to fight an evil Shade... I mean, who'd want to do anything else on a Saturday evening!"

Glancing at Ionie's happy face, Maia remembered something Sita had said – that she thought Ionie had been lonely and was really enjoying hanging around with them now they were all Star Friends. Maia was beginning to feel Sita was right.

When they went into the kitchen they found Maia's little brother, Alfie, sitting in his high chair.

"Morning, girls!" Mr Greene said cheerfully. "Nice to see you up so bright and early."

"We were going to go out for a bike ride," Maia said.

"OK, but have some breakfast first."

"Bek-fast!" called Alfie, offering his sister a piece of his toast.

Maia grinned. "Thanks, Alfie, but I'll get my own."

Alfie threw the toast on the floor. "All gone." He giggled.

"Come on, young man," Mr Greene said, undoing the harness and scooping Alfie up out of the high chair. "We're going to clear some leaves in the garden together."

Alfie shook his head firmly. "No leaves. No beetles."

"Don't be silly. Beetles won't hurt you," his dad said.

"No beetles! No!" Alfie's voice rose and he struggled in his dad's arms.

"He's scared of beetles," Maia explained to the others as they got out the cereal boxes. "He was helping Dad the other day and they found a nest of beetles under a pile of leaves."

"All right, Alfie, all right," Mr Greene said soothingly. "You can play in the sandpit then."

Alfie continued to struggle. "No garden! No!"

Sita went over and took his hands in hers. "Oh, Alfie, don't worry. The beetles will leave you alone. You can have a nice play in the sandpit." Alfie stopped wriggling and stared at her as she spoke. "You can play with your spade, can't you?" Sita went on, her gentle brown eyes fixed on his.

"Play," Alfie repeated, gazing at her. Then he looked up at his dad. "Me play outside."

Mr Greene blinked. "OK, great." He turned to Sita. "You really have a knack with little ones, Sita."

Sita smiled. "I get a lot of practice with my little brother."

Mr Greene nodded. "Well, thanks," he said, and he carried Alfie outside.

"Were you using your magic then?" Maia whispered to Sita.

She nodded and grinned. "Of course. Willow told me we should use it as often as we can to help people. Every bit of good we do strengthens the magic current."

"And our own magical abilities," added Ionie.

They had just started to eat breakfast when Mr Greene came back in.

"Maia, you haven't seen the key for the shed, have you?"

Maia shook her head. "Sorry, no."

Mr Greene frowned then went out again, muttering, "I don't know where it can be."

Maia thought for a second and then, remembering what Sita had said about using their magic to help people as much as they could, she picked up a spoon. Could she find the key? She turned over the spoon and looked into the shiny surface, opening her mind to the current of magic. She felt it flow into her, making her tingle all over.

"Show me the key to the shed," she whispered.

An image formed in the back of the spoon. It showed a key inside an old pottery vase. Maia recognized it as one of the flowerpots that sat just under the shelf where the key was usually kept. The key must have fallen into the vase!

She put down the spoon and hurried to the back door.

"Dad!" Her dad was looking under the jam jars and paint tins. "Have you tried in the flowerpots? It might have fallen off the shelf."

"I did have a quick look," Mr Greene said.

Maia's eyes fell on the vase, and she picked it up and turned it upside down. A metal key dropped out. "It's here! Look!"

"Oh, well done!" her dad said. "That was a lucky guess."

"Yep," Maia said, hiding her smile. Being able to do magic was awesome!

As soon as they had cleared away their bowls, the girls set off on their bikes. It was a crisp November morning and the sun was just starting to rise. The chilly breeze made their cheeks glow, and Maia was glad she had put on her scarf and gloves. The streets of Westcombe had an early Sunday morning quietness about them. A few people were out walking dogs or running but most of the houses still had their curtains drawn. The girls passed the playing fields where a huge bonfire was prepared.

"Are you all going to the fireworks tonight?" Maia asked as they cycled past.

Her friends nodded.

"How about we meet there at six?" Sita suggested.

"I can't be there until six fifteen," said Lottie. "Can we meet then? I'll be with my maths tutor until six."

Ionie frowned. "Maths tutor? Why do you have a maths tutor? You're almost as good at maths as me."

Maia groaned inwardly. Couldn't Ionie tell that saying things like that would really irritate Lottie?

"Because I'm sitting an entrance exam for secondary school in January and my mum wants me to try and get a scholarship," Lottie retorted. "And actually I'm *just* as good at maths as you!"

"Oh, look, there's Auntie Mabel's house," Maia said hurriedly, before Ionie could reply. "Maybe we should stop by later and tell her what happened last night."

Auntie Mabel was an old lady who could do magic – not with a Star Animal but by using crystals. She had been one of Maia's granny's best friends but Granny Anne had died just a few months ago. Auntie Mabel had told Maia that she knew all about Star Animals because she had seen Granny Anne's Star Animal – a wolf – when they were children. Auntie Mabel had said that she and Granny Anne used to do magic together and now she wanted to help Maia and her friends. Bracken and the other Star Animals weren't too keen on having the help of someone who wasn't a Star Friend but Maia really liked being able to talk to Auntie

Mabel about magic and ask for her advice.

"Shall we see if she's in now?" Ionie asked.

"It's still quite early," said Maia. "I'll call by and see her later."

The girls cycled across the main road and headed on to the track that led down through the wooded valley to the shingle beach. Seagulls swooped overhead and they could hear the distant sound of the sea. The path to the clearing was halfway down the track, opposite Granny Anne's cottage.

The girls left their bikes in the front garden. The cottage was empty now – Maia's parents had gradually been clearing out all her granny's things. Brambles caught at their legs as they pushed their way along the overgrown path and the air smelled of fallen leaves and damp.

Emerging into the clearing they called their animals' names. The four Star Animals appeared instantly. Bracken jumped round Maia, yapping excitedly. Juniper scampered up a tree. Willow cantered about, making playful little leaps, and Sorrel rubbed against Ionie's legs, purring loudly.

Maia kneeled down and Bracken jumped on to her lap, licking her cheeks and snuffling at her ears. She hugged his warm body. "It's magic time," she told him.

"I wonder if you'll be able to do anything new," he said.

Maia grinned and pulled a small mirror out of her pocket. "Only one way to find out.

I'm going to try looking into the past." It was something she had tried to do before but had never managed.

Ionie overheard. "Remember to relax!" she called.

"I will, thanks," Maia said gratefully. When she'd been struggling with her magic the week before, Ionie had given Maia some tips that had really worked.

Maia remembered Ionie's advice as she looked into the mirror. Breathe in for five seconds, hold her breath for five seconds, breathe out. Do that again and again. Count backwards from ten. She felt a sense of calm settle over her. Bracken snuggled against her legs and Maia stared at the mirror, letting everything else fade away…

The surface of the mirror shimmered. What did she want to see?

"Show me Granny Anne," she breathed. "Show me her with her Star Animal."

To her excitement an image appeared in
the mirror's surface. It was a young teenager
dressed in old-fashioned clothes –
brown trousers tucked into
socks and sturdy shoes, a
brown V-neck jumper
and blond hair held
back by a headscarf.
It was Granny Anne!
Maia recognized
her granny from old
photos she had seen.
Granny Anne was in
the woods and a slim silver
wolf with indigo eyes was at
her side. One of her hands was resting
on the wolf's back and in the other she held a
small mirror. Maia caught her breath. It was the
same mirror she was holding now – Granny
Anne had given it to her a year ago.

Her fingers tightened as she wondered if her

granny had suspected that she was also going to be a Star Friend. She'd talked to her so often about magic. Warmth flooded through her as she imagined how pleased her granny would be if she knew that Maia *was* a Star Friend now.

She let the image fade.

"Did you see your granny?" Bracken asked eagerly.

"Yes," she said. "She was with her Star Animal."

Bracken jumped round her. "This is brilliant, Maia. Your magic really *has* got stronger!"

Maia looked around, wondering what the others were doing. Sita was talking to Willow, Lottie seemed to have vanished and Ionie was standing in front of... Maia frowned. A table? What was a table doing in the clearing? It had a faint glowing outline.

"Ionie!" she called.

Ionie glanced over but before Maia could say anything, she felt a hand tug her hair. She jumped. Lottie was standing behind her.

Maia blinked. "How did you get there?"

"I can run so fast I'm invisible," Lottie said with a grin.

Maia gaped. "That's awesome!"

"I would hardly describe it as *awesome*," Sorrel commented with a dismissive flick of her tail. "In my opinion, the ability to run fast has only limited uses."

"Oh, really," said Lottie. She leaped forwards and disappeared. Two seconds later, Lottie was standing beside her again and Ionie was patting the side of her head in confusion. Lottie held out her hand to Maia. In her palm was Ionie's hairslide. "I think being able to run fast has quite a lot of uses," Lottie said.

The table vanished. Sorrel hissed at Lottie. "You made Ionie lose her concentration."

"What was she trying to do?" Maia asked. "Why was there a table there?"

"She was casting a glamour," said Bracken,

bounding over to where Ionie was standing.

"Correct!" said Sorrel smugly. "Now that is *definitely* an awesome ability."

"What's a glamour?" Maia asked.

Sorrel sighed. "A glamour is when magic is used to create an illusion. Something appears but really there's nothing there."

"A glamour can also disguise something," added Juniper.

Ionie's eyes shone. "I hadn't been able to do it when I'd tried before but now I can! Look!" She concentrated again and a chair appeared.

"That looks so real," breathed Sita. "That's an amazing power, Ionie."

Ionie looked delighted.

"It is, though the glowing light makes it just a little bit obvious that it's an illusion," Maia pointed out.

"What glowing light?" said Sita, looking surprised.

Bracken nudged Maia's hand with his nose. "Maia, I think you can see the light because your magic abilities are to do with sight. To everyone else it looks like a normal chair."

"Oh," said Maia.

Lottie linked arms with her. "I think it's just as cool to be able to see through illusions as to make them," she said, with a pointed look at Ionie.

"It will be a very useful ability," Bracken agreed. "The key to shattering an illusion is to refuse to believe it's real."

Maia looked at the chair. "You're not real," she

said. The chair vanished. "Whoops, sorry, Ionie!"

"It's OK, I can make it come back again," said Ionie. The chair reappeared.

"I don't believe in you," Maia said. It vanished again.

Ionie giggled. For a few moments, they kept making the chair appear and disappear then Ionie stopped. "I know, I want to try something else with my magic." She went and stood near to a patch of shadows and beckoned for Maia to join her. "Come here, Maia. I need your help with this."

Maia went over curiously. What was Ionie planning?

"Want to try and shadow-travel together?" Ionie asked.

"You can take me with you?" Maia said in surprise. Maia had seen Ionie transport herself from one place to another using shadows but it hadn't occurred to her that Ionie's magic could extend to other people.

"I'm not sure … but I'd like to have a go!" Ionie's green eyes shone. "My magic feels much stronger today." She took Maia's hand. "Just relax." She stepped into the shadows. Maia stepped with her and the world suddenly disappeared. The next second she was staggering slightly as everything came back into view. She blinked. They were on the other side of the clearing!

"Oh, Ionie, you exceptional girl!" exclaimed Sorrel in delight.

Ionie grinned. "Did you see?" she called to Sita and Lottie.

"Yes," said Lottie shortly.

"That's brilliant, Ionie," said Sita enthusiastically. She frowned slightly. "Everyone seems to have got new powers apart from me."

"Healing is a wonderful power on its own," Willow told her. "I'm sure your magic will be stronger and you'll be able to heal bigger wounds."

"Willow's right," Ionie said, going over to Sita. "And you're really good at calming people down and making them relax, too."

Sita smiled at her. "Thanks. I wouldn't want to be the one with the mega-power anyway."

"I wonder which of us it will be," said Ionie thoughtfully.

"Well," Sorrel began, "as I've already said, I think—" She was interrupted by a rustle in the trees.

"Someone's coming!" said Bracken.

The animals all vanished and the girls watched warily. Who was coming into the clearing?

CHAPTER THREE

An old woman hurried through the trees.
Her grey hair was cut very short and she was
wearing a scruffy beige raincoat and green
walking shoes. She had a wicker basket covered
with an old towel on one arm.

She froze as she saw the girls. "What are you
doing here?"

The girls looked at each other, taken aback
by her sharp tone.

"Um … we just came here for a walk,"
said Maia.

"Leaving litter, no doubt!" snapped the woman. She spotted an empty Coke can on the floor and scooped it up. "See! I knew it!"

"That's not ours," said Maia. She'd noticed it earlier and had planned to put it into a bin on the way home.

"A likely story!" snorted the woman. "You kids should clear off! Stay out of these woods."

"OK … um … we'll go then," said Maia, glancing at the others.

They backed away and hurried down the footpath.

"What a weird old woman!" hissed Lottie as soon as they were out of earshot.

"I didn't like her," said Sita with a shiver.

"I've never seen her before. Maybe she's just

visiting Westcombe," said Maia.

Westcombe was a large village but she knew most of the older people who lived there by sight.

"I think she's moved here," said Ionie. "I've seen her coming out of the cottage next door to your auntie Mabel's a few times. The one that was for sale in the summer."

Maia's heart sank. "Well, if she has moved in, I hope we don't see much of her."

Just then Maia's phone buzzed. It was a text from her mum.

> Dad says ur all out for a bike ride. If u want a hot choc then come to the Copper Kettle at 10.15. We'll be there with Alfie and Clio. Mum xxx

It was just past 10.15am. "Mum and Dad are at the Copper Kettle. If we meet them there they'll buy us a hot chocolate. Shall we go?"

The Copper Kettle was a cosy tea shop on the main road. The friends left their bikes in the bike rack and headed inside. The bell tinkled and they were hit with the smell of freshly bakes cakes and warm coffee. Maia breathed in deeply. "Mmm."

Her mum and dad were sitting with Alfie and Clio, Maia's fifteen-year-old sister, at a window table. Alfie was colouring in and Clio was flicking through a celebrity magazine while Mr and Mrs Greene were drinking their coffees.

"Mai-Mai!" cried Alfie.

Clio glanced up briefly from her magazine before carrying on reading.

"Pull up some chairs, girls," said Mr Greene.

Maia and her friends squeezed in round the table. Mary, the Copper Kettle's cheerful owner, bustled over to meet them. She was short and plump with curly brown hair and a beaming smile.

"What can I get you, girls?"

"Four hot chocolates I think, please, Mary," said Mrs Greene, looking at the girls who all nodded.

"What about cakes?" Mr Greene said.

Maia and Ionie asked for a slice of chocolate fudge cake each, Lottie chose a white chocolate brownie and Sita asked for lemon drizzle cake. Soon they were sipping mugs of hot chocolate topped with whipped cream and tiny pink and white marshmallows, and nibbling their cakes.

"I told your mum we'd be here," Mrs Greene said to Lottie. "She's going to call in to pick up you and Sita. I've got your sleeping bags and things in the car."

Alfie had finished colouring and started trying to grab handfuls of the leaflets that Mary displayed on the windowsill.

"Put them down, Alfie," said Mr Greene. "Have this instead." He handed Alfie a toy train, which he took happily, throwing the leaflets on the floor.

Maia picked up the leaflets. As she did so, she noticed one she hadn't seen before. "Look, this is for a new wildlife sanctuary," she said, showing it to her mum.

"We could go one weekend," Mrs Greene suggested.

Mary overheard them. "You really should visit the sanctuary," she said. "My sister Jenny moved into the village a month or so ago and now she works there. She said they have hedgehogs, squirrels, foxes and badgers. They take in animals that have been injured and nurse them back to health."

"We'll definitely go," said Maia to the others, who nodded.

"I'd like to run a wildlife sanctuary when I'm older," said Sita.

"Me, too," said Maia.

"I want to work with endangered animals all over the world," said Ionie.

"And I want to be a vet," said Lottie.

They talked about all the things they would do when they were older until Lottie's mum arrived.

"See you at the bonfire tonight," Maia said, as Lottie and Sita put their bikes into the boot of her car.

"Six fifteen," Lottie reminded everyone.

Maia turned to her mum and dad. "I might call in and see Auntie Mabel on the way home. Is that OK?"

"That's nice of you," her mum said. "Tell Auntie Mabel I'll pop over to visit her soon."

Maia was relieved her mum didn't want to come along – she had been hoping she would have the chance to talk to Auntie Mabel alone. She and Ionie got their bikes and rode down the road, then Ionie went on to her house and Maia turned into Auntie Mabel's street.

Getting off her bike, Maia leaned it against the wall outside Auntie Mabel's house.

A delivery man was knocking at the door of the cottage next to Auntie Mabel's. He was carrying a large cardboard box. The front door opened and a white dog ran out.

"Jack! Come here!" shouted a voice.

The dog only had one ear and half its tail was missing but Maia didn't care. She loved all animals. She went to the top of the drive to stop the dog running out on to the road and held out her hand but the dog backed away, growling. Maia was surprised. Animals usually liked her.

"It's all right," she murmured to the dog. "I'm not scary."

The dog directed a volley of barks in her direction.

The delivery man gave the dog a nervous look. "He doesn't seem too friendly, does he?"

Just then Maia noticed a woman with short grey hair at the door. It was the lady from the woods!

"Stay away from my dog!" the lady snapped at Maia. "Clear off with you!"

Maia backed away as the old lady called the dog into the house and snatched the parcel from the delivery man, slamming the door behind her. To Maia's relief, Auntie Mabel answered the front door on her first knock.

"Maia, how lovely to see you! I was just making some treacle toffee to take to bonfire night. Are you all right?" she asked, looking at Maia's flustered face.

"Yes." Maia swallowed. She didn't like being shouted at.

"What's the matter?" asked Auntie Mabel, ushering her in.

When Maia told her what had just happened, Auntie Mabel patted her hand. "Oh, my dear, how horrible. I didn't like Mrs Crooks the moment she moved in. She's done some very strange things. She had a large shed built in the garden and then put up a really high fence. She hardly says a word if I see her, even though I've asked her a few times if she wants to come to church or to coffee mornings. She's always going off into the woods at very bizarre times, too." She shook her head. "She's most peculiar."

Maia felt relieved it wasn't only the Star Friends thinking the old lady was odd.

Auntie Mabel led Maia through to the lounge. The surfaces were decorated with large shining crystals and a stone bowl that had some glittering polished stones inside. "I'm afraid I haven't managed to find out anything more about this Shade that's causing all the trouble."

"Oh, you needn't worry about that any more," said Maia, remembering she had good news. "It's been sent back to the shadows."

They sat down and Maia told Auntie Mabel everything that had happened the night before.

"Goodness me," said Auntie Mabel, putting her hand to her chest. "You all did very well.

However did you manage?"

"It was Ionie," said Maia. "She's a Spirit Speaker."

"I see," said Auntie Mabel thoughtfully. "Well, that's lucky for you. What about the others? You've never told me what they can do."

"Lottie has powers to do with agility and Sita is good at healing." As Maia spoke, she felt a bit uncomfortable. She knew Bracken didn't like her telling Auntie Mabel things about the magic – he had been told that no one apart from Star Friends should know anything.

Glancing round the room, she decided to change the subject. "Auntie Mabel," she said. "How do you do magic with crystals?"

"Well, crystals and stones contain their own special energy. I hold them in my hands and by concentrating hard I can use it – a bit like you drawing on the magic current. Different crystals and stones can do different things – some can heal, others see into the future, some will help calm an angry soul and others bring good luck. I've spent my life working out how to use their power."

"Is there any other type of magic – apart from Crystal Magic and Star Magic?" Maia asked curiously.

"There's dark magic, of course, when people draw power from the shadows," Auntie Mabel shuddered. "I don't like even thinking about that. And some people can draw magic from plants – they gather herbs and plants and make potions." She smiled. "If you hadn't met a Star Animal, then maybe you would have discovered how to use magic in another way. In fact, I'm sure you could master Crystal Magic. Here." She went to the stone bowl and pulled out a glittering round pink stone from the bottom. It seemed to glow with a faint golden light. "This is a Seeing Stone – let's see if I'm right." She held it out.

As Maia took the pretty crystal sphere, her fingers prickled and she caught her breath.

Auntie Mabel's eyebrows rose. "I can see you're feeling the magic. Seeing Stones can be used to look into the past. You told me you've been trying to do that with your own magic. Well, try with this. Just hold it, concentrate on it and tell it what you want to see."

It was on the tip of Maia's tongue to tell Auntie Mabel that she had finally managed to see into the past, but then there was a knock on the door.

"Oh, that will be my friends from the church hall committee," said Auntie Mabel. "We're having a knitting party this morning to make Christmas tree decorations to sell at the Christmas Fayre." She nodded at the stone. "Slip that in your pocket, dear. You can keep it."

Maia put the pink stone into her pocket. "Thank you! I'd better go now."

"Are you and your friends going to the bonfire tonight?" Auntie Mabel asked.

"Yes," said Maia.

"I'll see you all there then," Auntie Mabel said.

Maia followed her into the hall and Auntie Mabel opened the door to three ladies, all with baskets of wool and knitting needles.

"Hello, dear," said Margaret, who was tall and slim and used to play badminton with Granny Anne. "How are you?"

"Fine, thank you," Maia said.

"What are you up to today?" asked Josie, who ran the village playgroup and had known Maia since she was tiny.

"Oh, lots of different things," said Maia. "I'd better go. Bye, Auntie Mabel!" she called hastily, before the ladies invited her to stay and do some knitting!

Picking up her bike, she turned round and then froze. Two garden gnomes had appeared on either side of Mrs Crooks's front door. Garden gnomes that looked just like the gnome the horrible Wish Shade had been trapped in!

CHAPTER FOUR

Maia's heart thudded in her chest. The gnomes
had rosy red cheeks, little pointed hats and
big smiles. They looked just like the gnome
the Wish Shade had been in except one had a
fishing rod and one had a rabbit in its arms. She
had to investigate! Might these gnomes have
Shades in, too?

She checked no one was around and,
leaving her bike against the wall, she headed
up the path. She crouched down beside them
and poked them gingerly with a finger.

The front door
flew open. "You again!
What are you doing
with my new gnomes?"
said Mrs Crooks, coming
out on to the doorstep.

"Um... I... I ... was
just looking at them,"
Maia gabbled, jumping to
her feet. "They're really cute."

Mrs Crooks's eyes narrowed.
"Don't you go getting any idea about stealing
them."

Maia was shocked. "I wouldn't."

Mrs Crooks glared at her. "You stay away,"
she warned.

Maia backed off up the drive. Then, jumping
on her bike, she cycled away as quickly as she
could. Her thoughts were spinning as fast as
the wheels on her bike. What was Mrs Crooks
doing with those gnomes?

Icy fingers trailed down her spine. Could Mrs Crooks be the person doing dark magic? Maia was so busy thinking about it that she almost didn't notice Paige bouncing on the trampoline in her front garden.

"Hi, Maia!" Paige called, waving and then turning a somersault.

Maia skidded to a halt, remembering that they had been planning on asking Paige where the Wish Shade gnome had come from. "Hi, Paige. Are you OK today?"

Paige looked puzzled. "Yes, why?"

Maia lowered her voice. "After what happened with the gnome last night?"

Paige frowned. "The gnome? What do you mean?"

Maia realized that when the Shade had been sent back to the shadows, the magic must have made Paige forget everything about it. The same had happened to her sister, Clio, when they had sent back the Mirror Shade. "Don't worry," she said quickly. "But um … just one thing. You know the garden gnome that used to be here?"

"Yeah." Paige looked around. "Mummy must have moved it."

"Do you know where it came from?" Maia asked hopefully.

"One of Mummy's friends gave it to us," Paige said. "She brought it round and put it in the garden. It was a lady with grey hair… I can't remember her name. I think it was a present to say thank you to Mummy for helping with something or other." She grinned. "Mummy said she'd rather have had some chocolates!"

Maia's heart beat faster. Mrs Crooks had grey hair! "Are you sure you can't remember her name?" There were quite a few ladies with grey hair in the village.

Paige shook her head. "No. Why?"

"Oh, it was just that I thought I might get

one like him for my dad," Maia fibbed. "If you remember the lady's name, will you let me know?"

"Yep," said Paige, starting to bounce on the trampoline again. "I will. I think Mummy said she was a friend from church."

Maia said goodbye and carried on towards home. Mrs Crooks had grey hair but Auntie Mabel had said that Mrs Crooks had turned down her invitation to go to church with her. Had Mrs Crooks given the Wish Gnome to Paige's family or was it someone else? Maybe someone who hadn't known there was a Shade trapped inside it? Maia turned things over in her mind and cycled faster. She had to get home so she could talk to Bracken. She was sure Mrs Crooks was involved – but how?

✦ ✦ ✦

As soon as Maia reached her bedroom, she shut the door and whispered Bracken's name. He appeared in front of her, bouncing round and wagging his bushy tail. Maia sat on the bed and he jumped up beside her.

"What's been happening?" he asked. He always seemed to know when she had things that she needed to talk about.

"I saw Paige," Maia said quickly. "She can't remember the name of the person who gave the Wish Gnome to her mum but she said it was a lady from church. But that's not all – there's an old lady who has moved in next to Auntie Mabel. She's really weird and has a very strange dog and when I came out of Auntie Mabel's house, I saw two gnomes on her doorstep. Two gnomes just like the Wish Gnome!"

Bracken barked in alarm.

"Could she be the person who's doing dark magic?" Maia said.

"She might be planning to put Shades inside the gnomes," said Bracken anxiously.

"That Shade in my dream said more Shades

had been called from the shadows. I'd better tell the others." Maia reached for her phone but then paused. It was too risky to send a text just in case one of their parents checked their phone. "I'll tell them tonight at the bonfire," she decided. "If only Paige could remember the name of the person who gave the gnome to her mum!"

"Maybe you could use your magic to find out," Bracken said thoughtfully. "I know it didn't work when you asked to see who trapped the Shade inside the gnome... But how about asking it to show you who *gave* the gnome."

"That's a great idea!" Maia said. She put her hand in her pocket to pull out the mirror and her fingers brushed against the round pink stone that Auntie Mabel had given her. She decided not to tell Bracken about it – she had a feeling he wouldn't approve of Auntie Mabel suggesting she try doing magic in other ways. Leaving the stone in her pocket, she took out the mirror.

"Show me the moment the Wish Gnome arrived at Paige's house," she whispered.

The surface swirled with light and an image appeared in the glass. Maia peered at it eagerly. She caught sight of a figure in a long coat but then, to her disappointment, the image blurred.

"Show me who gave the Wish Gnome to Paige's family," she whispered again.

But the image stayed blurry. "It's not working today," she said to Bracken. "I can't see clearly."

He licked her cheek. "Have a rest and try again later," he said.

Maia tried again several times that day but

each time the mirror failed to show her what she wanted to see. In the end she had to give up and get ready to go out for the fireworks.

"Have fun," Bracken said, licking her nose. "I'll see you when you get home."

Maia hugged him and then he vanished. As she took off her jeans to change for the bonfire, the Seeing Stone Auntie Mabel had given her fell out of her pocket. She picked it up. It was so pretty. Would she really be able to do magic with it?

She stroked the stone and felt the magic in it prickle her fingers. Maybe she could use it to see who had given the gnome to Paige's family. What had Auntie Mabel told her she needed to do?

No. She stopped herself. It felt wrong to try and do magic with the stone without telling Bracken. Reluctantly she put it down on her desk. She would tell Bracken about it later and together they could decide what she should do.

CHAPTER FIVE

The night was cold and frosty, and the air was full of the smell of smoke as Maia walked up to the playing fields with her family. She usually liked the smell of woodsmoke but now it made her think about the Wish Shade trying to burn down the shed in Paige's garden with her, Lottie and Sita all locked inside. Horrible pictures flashed through her mind – the Wish Shade they had fought, the gnomes outside Mrs Crooks's house, the dream she had had about more Shades coming...

She spotted Lottie, Sita and Ionie by the scout hut and told her mum she was going to meet them. "We need to talk," she hissed, as she hurried over.

"What about?" Ionie said.

Sita's eyes widened. "Did you see Paige?"

Maia nodded but before she could say anything she was interrupted.

"Hello, girls," Auntie Mabel said. She took some packets of sparklers out of her handbag. "Maia said you'd be here so I thought I'd bring you all a little present. There's a pack each."

"Thanks, Auntie Mabel," said Maia.

"I love sparklers," Ionie said. "Thank you!"

"Look, the packs have got a free gift with them!" said Sita. Each pack of sparklers had a little yellow stretchy man sellotaped on to it.

"Cool!" said Lottie.

Auntie Mabel peered at them. "How strange. I don't remember seeing those when I bought them."

Lottie took the little man off her pack and waggled its legs and arms. "Do you remember the craze at school when all the boys had these? They kept throwing them at the walls to stick and the teachers got really cross."

Just then Maia's mum and dad walked over with Alfie on Mr Greene's shoulders. "Hi, girls, do you want some sparklers?" asked Mrs Greene.

Maia's heart sank. Now there was no way she would get a chance to talk to the others. "It's OK, thanks. Auntie Mabel's just given us some," she said.

"That's really kind of you, Mabel," said Mrs Greene.

"It's no problem at all, dear. Now I'd better go and help with the teas and coffees. Enjoy the fireworks, all of you!"

With a cheerful wave, Auntie Mabel disappeared into the scout hut.

"Mabel's getting a lot more involved with village life than she used to," Mrs Greene said to Mr Greene.

"She must be lonely without Granny Anne," he said. "They used to spend so much time together, didn't they?"

"Well, I'm glad she's keeping busy," said Mrs Greene.

Alfie suddenly spotted the stretchy man in Lottie's hands. "Me! Me!" he said, reaching out.

"No. They belong to the girls, Alfie," said Mrs Greene.

"Me want!" Alfie's voice rose.

"It's OK, he can have mine," said Maia,

taking the stretchy man off her packet of
sparklers and giving it to her brother.

Just then there was a shrill sound and a
crackle as multicoloured stars exploded into the
dark sky.

"The fireworks are starting!" said Mrs Greene.

Ionie pulled Maia slightly away from the
adults. "You were going to tell us something,"
she whispered.

The fireworks exploded overhead with a
bang and a fountain of silver and gold stars.
Maia shook her head. It was far too
noisy to talk now and there
were people everywhere.

"I'll tell you tomorrow,"
she hissed. "Let's meet in
the playground before
school starts."

Ionie nodded and
another firework
erupted in the sky.

Maia woke early the next morning. To her relief, she hadn't had another nightmare about the Shades.

She glanced at her clock. There was still half an hour before she needed to get up for school. Bracken was snoozing beside her, his body stretched out along the duvet, his snout resting on her arm. She stroked his head and he wriggled up the bed and nuzzled her cheek with his cold nose. She giggled. "That tickles!"

Bracken rolled on to his back so she could scratch his tummy. "What are we doing today?" he asked.

"I've got school." Maia sighed. She glanced at her desk and saw the round pink stone there, glowing faintly in the dim light. She went over and picked it up.

"What have you got there?" Bracken asked.

"It's a Seeing Stone." Maia felt awkward.

"Auntie Mabel gave it to me yesterday. She said I can use it to look into the past."

"But you don't need a Seeing Stone," said Bracken. "You can look into the past using the Star Magic."

"I didn't get a chance to tell her I'd managed to do that," said Maia. "Maybe I should just try with this stone… It might be easier." She gave him a hopeful look.

"Don't," Bracken said uneasily. "It doesn't feel right to me. You're a Star Friend. You should use Star Magic."

"OK," Maia said. She sat down at her desk and dropped the stone into her lap. "I'll try this mirror again." She stared at the mirror on her desk and asked it to show her who put the gnome in Paige's garden.

But just like the day before, the image flickered and was too blurry to see properly.

"It's no good." Maia glanced at her bedside clock. "Why don't I have a quick try with the stone? Auntie Mabel thought it would help."

"All right," Bracken said, but he didn't sound happy about it.

Maia picked the stone out of her lap and gazed at it. "Show me the day the gnome arrived at Paige's house," she whispered. Excitement flared inside her as an image started to form inside it. Bracken paced round her chair but Maia hardly noticed, she was far too busy staring at the image. Auntie Mabel was right, she could do other types of magic! It felt different though – as if her energy was being pulled into the pink stone.

She saw a woman in a raincoat with the hood pulled up, standing in the driveway of Paige's house by the trampoline. The person's back was to Maia but then she half-turned. Maia gasped as she saw the Wish Gnome in her hands. She still couldn't see the woman's face properly but after she placed the gnome on the ground and straightened up, the hood of the coat fell back revealing short iron-grey hair and a familiar face.

"Mrs Crooks!" exclaimed Maia. She lowered the stone in shock. "Bracken! It was Mrs Crooks!"

CHAPTER SIX

"I knew I didn't like that lady when I saw her in the woods," said Lottie, as they huddled together in a far corner of the playground later that morning. Their breath was freezing in icy clouds on the air.

Maia nodded. "Mrs Crooks hasn't been in the village long and the Shades only started appearing recently, too!"

"And there are two gnomes on her doorstep?" said Sita.

Maia nodded. "Yes, and she's the person who

gave the Wish Gnome to Paige's mum! I saw her with my magic. Paige must have been mistaken when she said it was a lady from the church."

"She has to be the one doing dark magic," said Ionie.

Sita looked worried. "What if she puts Wish Shades into lots more gnomes and gives them to more people? Imagine lots of people making wishes that are granted in a horrible way."

"We don't know for sure that Mrs Crooks *is* the person who is conjuring Shades," Lottie pointed out. "We really need proof."

"I could try spying on her house through my mirror," Maia said. "I might see something that would prove she's using dark magic."

"Why don't you all ask if you can come to mine after school?" said Ionie. "If Maia can't see anything, I could shadow-travel to Mrs Crooks's house."

"That's too dangerous!" Sita protested.

"I can't meet tonight," said Lottie. "I've got gymnastics."

"We shouldn't do anything without Lottie," said Sita quickly. "It's not fair."

Maia glanced at Lottie. She didn't want to leave her out but if Ionie was right about there being more Shades, they had to do something fast. "Do you want us to wait until tomorrow?" she asked Lottie.

"No," Lottie said reluctantly. "You should find out what's going on. Tomorrow I have piano so I won't be able to meet up then either. I'm not free after school until Wednesday. But promise you'll tell me everything?"

"Promise. I'll call by your house tonight and fill you in," said Sita.

"All right then. Be careful, all of you," Lottie told them.

Maia took a deep breath. "We will."

After school, the girls shut themselves in Ionie's bedroom and called their animals. They sat on the floor and Maia took out her pocket mirror. She felt the magic tingle through her.

Show me inside Mrs Crooks's house, she thought.

An image appeared of a kitchen. There was a wooden table and two chairs, a dresser with some neatly stacked wildlife magazines and a lot of brightly coloured plastic bowls on the draining board. Maia felt a flicker of disappointment. She wasn't quite sure what she had been expecting.

"I can see the kitchen," Maia told the others. "It just looks normal, though…" She broke off as the image in the mirror showed a door open. Mrs Crooks came in, with the one-eared white dog at her heels.

"Time to go and check on the shed," she heard Mrs Crooks saying. "They'll be ready to go soon."

Maia's eyes widened. *They'll be ready to go soon.* What was Mrs Crooks talking about?

Mrs Crooks bent down and stroked the dog's head. "One day, they'll all be set free. That's what we want, isn't it?" The ugly little dog ran to the back door and whined. Mrs Crooks smiled. "All right. Let's go and see my beauties." She opened the back door and they went out.

Maia slowly lowered the mirror.

"Well?" Ionie demanded.

Maia's mouth felt dry. "Mrs Crooks was talking to her dog about something she keeps in the shed. She said 'they'll be ready to go soon' and something about setting them free."

Sita looked worried. "Do you think she's got some Shades in her shed?"

"Can you look inside it?" Ionie asked quickly.

"I'll try." Maia picked up the mirror again. *Inside Mrs Crooks's shed*, she thought.

An image appeared. There was no light in the shed and blinds were drawn across the windows, but Maia could just about make out some boxes. No. Not boxes. They were metal and wire-mesh cages. "There are cages in the shed!" Maia said to the others.

Sorrel hissed. "We need to investigate this more!"

Bracken leaped to his feet. "I agree! We need to look inside this shed properly."

"We might be able to spy on it from Auntie Mabel's garden," said Maia. "Or even climb over the fence and get inside."

"Or shadow-travel inside," put in Ionie.

"But what if there *are* Shades in there?" said Sita. "They might attack us. They've got such sharp nails and they move so fast and—"

"Sita!" Maia put a hand on her arm. "Calm down."

Willow nuzzled Sita. "Don't be scared. We have to find out what's going on. It's what Star Friends do."

Sita took a trembling breath. "I know. I just hate Shades."

Maia squeezed her arm. "Don't worry. We'll all be together. Nothing bad will happen."

I hope, she added in her head.

CHAPTER SEVEN

Auntie Mabel answered the door. "Hello, girls," she said in surprise.

"Please can we come in, Auntie Mabel?" Maia said. "We need to use your garden."

Auntie Mabel raised her eyebrows but ushered them inside. "So what's this about?" she asked as she shut the door.

"We think Mrs Crooks might be the person conjuring the Shades," said Maia.

"No!" Auntie Mabel gasped.

Maia nodded and told Auntie Mabel about

the image of Mrs Crooks with the gnome in Paige's garden. She explained what she had heard Mrs Crooks saying and told her about the cages in the shed.

"I never liked that woman," said Auntie Mabel, shaking her head.

"We need to try and find out exactly what's in her shed," said Ionie. "Can we use your garden please?"

"Of course. You can call your Star Animals, too, if you want," said Auntie Mabel. "After all, it's not like you have to keep them secret from me!"

"Thank you!" Maia said. She would feel much happier if they could have Bracken, Sorrel and Willow with them.

They hurried through the house and out of the back door to the garden. They whispered the names of their animals, and Bracken, Sorrel and Willow appeared.

Maia heard Auntie Mabel's intake of breath

and saw the old lady looking at the animals with a strange expression.

Bracken shot Maia an uncertain look.

"Oh, don't you worry about me, dear," said Auntie Mabel, backing into the house. "I'll stay out of your way." She disappeared into the house and then reappeared at the kitchen window.

"Maia!" Bracken said anxiously. "You know people shouldn't see us unless they're Star Friends."

"It's only Auntie Mabel and she's seen Granny Anne's Star Animal. Don't worry," said Maia.

"I smell Shades," said Sorrel, scenting the air. Her tail fluffed up. "All around here."

Willow went to the fence that separated Auntie Mabel's garden from Mrs Crooks's. "I can smell it here."

"The fence is too high for us to see over," Maia said. "If only Lottie was here, she'd be able to climb the fence."

"Lottie isn't the only one who can climb," said Sorrel. She jumped up and dug her claws into the side of the fence. In a few seconds, she was balancing on the top. "I can see the shed," she told them. "It's just on the other side. I'll try and see through the windows." She jumped down into Mrs Crooks's garden.

Ionie stepped towards a nearby patch of shadows.

"No!" Sita said, grabbing her. "Don't

shadow-travel there, Ionie. It could be dangerous. Let's wait and see what Sorrel finds out."

Ionie looked like she was about to argue.

"Please stay," Sita repeated.

To Maia's surprise, Ionie gave way and nodded. "OK."

A few moments later, Sorrel reappeared at the top of the fence. "These gardens definitely smell of Shades," she said, jumping down and wrinkling her nose in distaste.

"What did you find out?" Ionie asked eagerly.

"Not a lot. I saw the cages through a gap in the shed wall but I couldn't see into them. Oh, and there are gnomes in the garden."

"Gnomes," Maia echoed.

"Yes. Just like that one the Wish Shade was in. Lots of them."

Maia shook her head. "This is weird."

"We need to get into that shed," said Ionie. "I'll shadow-travel into the garden and see if I can get inside."

Ionie stepped towards the shadows but, as she did so, Bracken's ears pricked up. "Wait! I hear the back door." He cocked his head to one side, listening. "Mrs Crooks has just come into the garden!"

Ionie looked at Maia. "What do we do? Maybe I could use an illusion – disguise myself in some way and get into the garden. Or I could shadow-travel here tonight and look into the shed then?"

"But you'd be on your own," Sita pointed out. "It's too risky." She took hold of Maia's and Ionie's hands. "Look, I know you both want to do something right now but remember how dangerous Shades are. And this time there might be lots of them. Please don't do anything just yet. Let's talk to Lottie and Juniper first."

Maia wanted to argue but maybe Sita was right. She found herself nodding and realized Ionie was nodding, too.

"All right," Ionie agreed.

"We'll wait," said Maia.

"OK, good," said Sita, looking relieved. "I'll tell Lottie what we've found out. And then we can think up a plan."

✦ ✦ ✦

Maia racked her brains but by bedtime she still hadn't thought of a way they could safely get into Mrs Crooks's garden and see inside the shed. She tried spying on Mrs Crooks but all she saw was her making an omelette and watching a wildlife programme on TV – nothing to suggest Mrs Crooks was doing dark magic.

As she snuggled down in bed that night, she pulled Bracken close. "I hope I don't have any horrible dreams tonight."

He licked her cheek. "I'll wake you if you do."

She kissed his head and went to sleep with him curled up against her tummy.

She didn't have a nightmare but her dreams were full of strange images again – Sita staring at a patch of shadows in alarm, Lottie pacing anxiously around her bedroom, Ionie sitting on her bed looking unhappy, a person in a hooded cloak, tiny figures scuttling through the shadows and a night sky where the stars formed into words: *her power grows.*

When Maia woke up, she rubbed her eyes and yawned. She felt tired even though she had just had a whole night's sleep. She wondered what the images meant, particularly the last one. Whose power was growing? Was it one of them or the person doing dark magic?

She gave Bracken a cuddle and then got up

and went downstairs.

Her mum was in the kitchen with Alfie on her lap.

"Morning," said Maia.

"Morning," said her mum, yawning.

"Are you all right?" Maia asked, thinking her mum looked just as tired as she felt.

"Alfie kept having nightmares," said Mrs Greene. "I think the fireworks must have upset him."

"Not fireworks. Beetle," said Alfie solemnly. He cuddled closer to Mrs Greene. "Big beetle." He looked at Maia with wide eyes and his lower lip trembled. "In my room!"

"It was just a bad dream, Alfie," Maia said. "There are no beetles in your room."

Alfie didn't look convinced. "Beetle," he said again.

"I know!" Maia hurried to the cupboard under the stairs where they kept all sorts of random things like gloves, umbrellas and picnic blankets. She rummaged on one of the shelves and found what she was looking for. A plastic bug catcher! She'd liked to play with it when she was little, pressing the lever and clamping the plastic jaws round her toys. She took it back to Alfie. "Here. If you see a beetle, you can pick it up with this and get rid of it." She picked a toy train off the floor to show him how it worked.

"Me do it!" Alfie wriggled off Mrs Greene's lap and took the bug catcher from Maia, his nightmare forgotten.

"Thanks, Maia," Mrs Greene said with a smile.

Maia made herself some breakfast then got ready for school. She desperately wanted to see the others. Maybe they had had some ideas. She sent them a text.

See u all at school before the bell! Mxx

A reply pinged back from Ionie almost instantly.

Definitely! Can't wait to see u! xxxxxxx ☺☺☺

Maia blinked. Ionie's texts were usually quite short and she almost *never* used that many kisses and emojis. What was going on?

Her mum dropped her off early. The school playground was still almost empty. Ionie was sitting on the wall at the edge of the playground. She came running over eagerly. "I thought you were never going to arrive!"

Maia was surprised. "It's still early."

"I know but I was worried." Ionie's face took on an anxious expression that was very out of character. "You do still want to be friends with me, don't you?"

"Of course. Why?" Maia said in astonishment.

"Oh, nothing." Ionie looked relieved. "It's just I had a dream last night that none of you wanted me to be a Star Friend. It felt so real." The anxious look crossed her face again. "It's not true, is it?"

"No," Maia reassured her. "Of course not. Everyone likes you. Although you might want to stop telling Lottie that you're better than she is at maths," she added. "I think that annoys her just a little bit."

Ionie looked horrified. "Oh no! I didn't mean to annoy her."

Maia was saved from replying by Sita arriving in the playground.

"Hi." Sita glanced over her shoulder as she reached them.

"Are you OK?" Maia said.

"Not really. I thought I saw something in the shadows when I was walking to school," whispered Sita. "It looked like a Shade!"

"A Shade!" echoed Maia and Ionie.

"I thought I saw one last night, too," Sita told them. "It was in my room when I turned off my light. It was there for a minute, right by my wardrobe, and then it disappeared."

Maia frowned. "What about Willow? Did she sense it?"

"I called her and when she appeared she said she could smell a Shade, but the scent was faint and it didn't seem to come from near the wardrobe. The Shade had seemed so real and—"

She was interrupted by Ionie suddenly waving madly. "Lottie, hi! Over here!" she called, as Lottie came into the playground. Lottie hurried over.

"Lottie! I never meant to upset you. I think you're brilliant at maths – really, really brilliant!" Ionie burst out.

Maia stared. It was like an over-friendly alien

had invaded Ionie's body! For a moment she wondered if it could be a Shade… But no, it wasn't making Ionie horrible. It was making her super-nice.

Lottie looked surprised.

"You really are so good at it," Ionie carried on.

"No, I'm not," said Lottie gloomily. "I couldn't sleep last night. I kept thinking about that inter-schools maths challenge we did. I'm sure I've done badly in it. I think I've failed my piano exam, too. What if I've failed them both? I'm dreading getting the results."

"You never fail anything," said Maia. "You'll be fine. Look, we need to think about Mrs Crooks. Did Sita tell you everything last night?"

Lottie nodded.

"We need to get a proper look inside that shed," said Maia. "Has anyone come up with any good ideas?"

"I bet you have," said Ionie, smiling at her. "You're so great at thinking up ideas, Maia."

"Well, I haven't thought of anything yet," Maia admitted. "Have you?"

Ionie shook her head.

"Sita?" Maia asked.

"What?" Sita jumped as Maia said her name.

"Have you had any ideas?" Maia said.

"About what? About the Shade that's following me?"

"No," said Maia. "I really don't think there's a Shade following you. About Mrs Crooks!"

"Oh … um … that," said Sita. "No, I haven't thought of anything."

"Me neither," said Lottie. "The only things I can think about are my piano exam and the maths challenge. I can't bear it if I've failed."

Maia felt like stamping her foot in frustration. Whatever was up with her friends that morning? They were being really strange.

By the time school had ended, Maia had come up with a plan. If she and Sita distracted Mrs Crooks at the front door, Ionie could shadow-travel into the garden, and try and see into the shed. However her plans were dashed when Ionie's mum told them that Ionie had a dentist appointment after school.

"I'll have to miss it, Mum," said Ionie. "We've got stuff planned."

"Oh no," her mum said. "You can't miss the dentist."

Ionie turned to Maia and Sita. "Don't do anything without me."

"We won't, we'll wait until tomorrow," Maia said. Even if they had wanted to, they needed Ionie's shadow-travelling to make the plan work.

"Lottie will be able to meet up with us tomorrow, too," said Sita.

"So you promise you won't go off and do anything without me?" said Ionie.

"I said we wouldn't!" Maia spoke slightly sharply.

"Now you're in a mood with me!" wailed Ionie.

"I'm not!"

"You are."

"Come on, Ionie," her mum insisted.

Ionie reluctantly left, shooting backward glances at her friends.

"I have no idea what's up with her today," Maia said to Sita.

"She is being odd," agreed Sita. "I'm glad we're not going to Mrs Crooks's house though. What if there are Shades in the shed?"

"Then we have to deal with them," said Maia firmly. "If Mrs Crooks is doing dark magic we have to stop her, Sita, you know we do."

Sita swallowed. "Y-yes. I guess."

Maia sighed. "I'll see you tomorrow."

"You're not going round to anyone's house today?" Mrs Greene said in surprise as Maia joined her. "That's unusual. How about we call in and see Auntie Mabel then?"

"OK," said Maia. "Where's Alfie?" she asked.

"At home with Dad. He had such a bad night's sleep, he didn't go to playgroup today. So how was school?"

"OK," said Maia, thinking about how strangely her friends had been behaving. She couldn't wait to get home and talk to Bracken

about it. Could it be because of some sort
of dark magic?

When they reached the row of cottages
where Auntie Mabel lived, Maia saw Mrs
Crooks's dog watching through her front
window. He barked when he saw her and Mrs
Crooks appeared. Seeing Maia, she scowled
and closed the curtains.

"Come on, Maia," her
mum called, as Auntie
Mabel answered her
front door.

"How lovely to
see you both. I've
got some friends
from church
here," said
Auntie Mabel.
"We're planning
the Christmas
Fayre."

"Oh, we won't bother you then," Mrs Greene said.

"No, no, come in and have a cup of tea with us. Please do."

Maia's heart sank. The ladies all greeted her and her mum warmly. Maia's family didn't go to church but Granny Anne had and the ladies had all been her friends.

"I'll just put the kettle on. Maia, would you like a hot chocolate?" Auntie Mabel said.

"Yes, please," said Maia.

"Why don't you come and give me a hand?" said Auntie Mabel.

Leaving her mum to chat, Maia went into the kitchen with her. "So," Auntie Mabel lowered her voice to a whisper and beckoned Maia closer. "Have you found out anything else about you-know-who?" She gestured towards Mrs Crooks's house.

"No," Maia whispered back. "Not yet."

"I've been watching her. She went out late

last night with a basket. I think she might be collecting herbs and plants to do magic with. Shades can be conjured using potions. Did you know that?"

Maia's heart beat faster. "No."

"We need to keep an eye on her," said Auntie Mabel. "She could have a secret place she goes to when she wants to work magic."

"In the woods, maybe?" Maia said.

"It's very likely," Auntie Mabel agreed, nodding. "I'll try and watch her using my crystals. Have you had a go at doing magic with the Seeing Stone I gave you?"

"Yes, it worked!" Maia said. "I saw into the past. That was how I saw Mrs Crooks with the gnome at Paige's."

Auntie Mabel smiled. "Well done. You're obviously very talented at magic."

Maia glowed. "Do you really think so?"

"Yes, I do," Auntie Mabel said. She gave her a curious look. "Why do you ask?"

"Well, it's just one of the Shades we fought said that one of us would be really powerful – more powerful than the person doing dark magic."

Auntie Mabel leaned closer. "Did the Shade say which of you it would be?"

"I don't know. He didn't—" Maia broke off as her mum came in.

Mrs Greene laughed as they both jumped. "What are you two whispering about?"

Auntie Mabel chuckled. "Oh, it's just a silly little secret we have," she said, tapping her nose and looking at Maia. "Isn't that right, Maia?"

Maia nodded.

Auntie Mabel smiled brightly at Mrs Greene. "Let's have some tea!"

CHAPTER EIGHT

Maia was keen to tell the others what Auntie Mabel had said about people being able to conjure Shades using potions, but when she got to school the next day, they were all still acting oddly. She found Lottie sitting on a bench, her head buried in her spelling book. "We've got a test today. I'm sure I'm going to fail," she muttered. "I can't talk now."

"Lottie, you're brilliant at spelling. You won't fail. I need to talk to you, this is important!" Maia said.

"Not as important as my test." Lottie got up. "You don't get it!" She ran off.

Before Maia could go after her, Sita arrived. Her eyes were wide and scared.

"Maia! I'm sure there's a Shade stalking me!" she hissed as she raced up to her. "It was in our garden this morning and then behind some trees on the way to school. One minute it's there, the next it's gone."

"Let's go to the wall and talk there," said Maia.

"OK, there's something else I need to talk to you about as well," said Sita. "I'm sure it's not true but Willow said I should mention it to you all."

As they walked over to the wall, Ionie came running up.

"Where are you two going? Why weren't you waiting for me? You don't like me, do you? I knew it!" Her eyes filled with tears as she looked from Maia to Sita.

"Don't be silly!" Maia said in astonishment.

"Ionie, I saw a Shade," said Sita.

"Where?" said Ionie.

"In the trees, in the garden…"

Maia sighed. "Sita thinks he's stalking her but…"

Ionie glared. "So you've been talking about it without me? Leaving me out?"

"No!" Maia protested.

"I knew you didn't want to be friends with me!" Ionie said, and fighting back a sob she hurried away.

"OK," Maia said in despair. "Why are you all behaving so strangely?"

"Look, in the shadows over there!" gasped Sita, pointing to a nearby hedge. Maia looked but there was nothing there. She let magic flow into her and used her powers to see if there was anything she couldn't detect with her normal vision. Nothing.

"Sita, there really isn't a Shade there," she said. "I'm sure of it."

The bell rang and Sita breathed a sigh of relief. "I'm going inside. It won't follow me there!"

Maia was beginning to think that somehow a Shade was affecting her friends. But what was it trying to do? Was there a type of Shade that just made people behave oddly? And if it was affecting her friends, why wasn't it affecting her?

Oh, Bracken, I wish I could talk to you right now! she thought.

After school, no one wanted to meet up. Lottie wanted to go home in case the postman had delivered her exam results, Ionie was still refusing to talk to Maia and Sita, and Sita said she wanted to stay with her mum.

As soon as Maia got home, she called Bracken.

"What is it?" he asked her. "You look upset."

Maia hugged him and told him what they had been doing in a rush.

"Why don't I go and talk to Willow, Sorrel and Juniper?" Bracken said. "If a Shade has been anywhere near the others, Sorrel and Willow will definitely have smelled it."

"Can you just go off and talk to them?" said Maia. A thought struck her.

"I can call them using Star Magic and we can meet each other if we go to the clearing," Bracken replied. "The clearing is special because Star Magic is strong there. The waterfall is a link between this world and the

Star World. I'll be back as soon as I can."

Maia kissed his head and he disappeared.

Once he had left, the minutes seem to drag by. She picked up her mirror. Maybe while she was waiting she should use her magic? But what would she ask to see?

Sita, she decided.

A picture of her friend appeared in the mirror. She was with Willow in her bedroom.

"I still haven't talked to the others about it, Willow," she was saying.

"You must," Willow said softly.

"But what do you think they'll say?" A noise made Sita jump. "The Shade! I just saw it again!"

"Sita, there's nothing there," said Willow.

Maia shook her head and tried Ionie next.

Ionie was sitting on her bed, her arms pulled tight round her knees. Sorrel was nudging her head against Ionie's arm.

"No one likes me, Sorrel," Ionie was saying.

"Maia and Sita keep going off and leaving me out."

We don't, Maia thought. *What's she talking about?*

"They don't want to be friends and Lottie's never liked me," Ionie went on. "I'm never going to have any real friends, am I?" She sounded so despairing. Her usual air of confidence had completely vanished.

"I'm your friend. I'll always be here for you," Sorrel said, her voice soft for once. "Please don't be upset, Ionie. This isn't like you." She nuzzled Ionie's cheek. Suddenly she stiffened, her head tilting to one side. "Ionie, Bracken is calling me. I need to go. He wouldn't be calling me unless it was important."

Maia let the image fade and tried Lottie. She was pacing around her bedroom. "I'm going to fail, I'm going to fail," she was whispering. "Oh, what am I going to do?"

Juniper wasn't there. Maia wondered if he

was with Bracken and the others in the woods.

Maia put down the mirror. Her friends all seemed so unhappy. She ran her hands through her hair. She didn't know what to do about her friends and she didn't know what to do about Mrs Crooks. Were the two things connected?

Maia felt like she had lots of pieces of a jigsaw laid out in front of her but she just couldn't seem to put the picture together.

A few minutes later, there was a shimmer of light and Bracken reappeared.

"I've spoken to the other animals, Maia."

"And?" Maia demanded.

"They all agree something strange is going on. Sorrel and Willow have both smelled the faint scent of dark magic in Ionie and Sita's bedrooms, although they say the smell comes and goes. They're worried."

"What do we do, Bracken?" Maia said. "Should we try and find out what's going on with them or should we try and find out more about Mrs Crooks? If only the others weren't so distracted."

Bracken yipped and pricked his ears. "Maia! Maybe that's it! If Mrs Crooks has somehow found out you're all Star Friends, she might be using magic to distract them."

Maia frowned. "But why just Lottie, Sita and Ionie? Surely she'd want to distract me, too."

Bracken's ears lowered. "Yes, you're right, that doesn't make sense," he admitted.

"Maia!" Clio called from outside the room. "Mum says tea is ready."

"Coming!" Maia got to her feet. "I'll be back as soon as I can," she promised Bracken.

Maia's mum had cooked lasagne for tea, Maia's favourite, but she was so worried about what was going on, she didn't feel like eating.

Alfie didn't seem to want his either. He pushed it round his plate and kept throwing his fork on the floor.

"Come on, Alfie, eat up," said Clio, picking up a spoonful of lasagne from his plate. "Here comes the train. Choo-choo!"

"No!" Alfie wailed, hitting out and sending the spoon flying.

Mrs Greene rubbed her forehead wearily. "Don't worry, Clio. He's just really tired." Standing up, she lifted Alfie out of his chair. "Let's go and get you into your pyjamas, Alfie-boy."

"I'll take him upstairs, Mum," offered Maia. Her mum looked really tired.

"Thanks, sweetie." Mrs Greene smiled. "Once he's got his PJs on, he can come down and have some milk and I'll read him a story."

Maia nodded and swung Alfie on to her hip. "Up we go," she said, heading for the door.

Alfie clutched her as they reached the stairs.

"Beetle! No!"

"What do you mean, beetle?" she said.

He struggled. "In my room. Beetle!"

"There aren't beetles in your room, Alfie. You just saw them in a nightmare."

"No." He shook his head. "Big beetle!"

They reached the top of the stairs. Maia put him down. "All right, if there's a big beetle, I'll get rid of it," she said. "Let me have a look." She pushed open the bedroom door. Alfie's room looked just like it usually did. "See, no beetles."

Alfie came slowly into the room. He stiffened and pointed at the wardrobe.

"Beetle!" he whispered, his eyes growing wide as saucers.

"Don't be silly, there isn't a—" Maia broke off with a squeak as a large black beetle leg appeared out of one of the wardrobe doors.

"Mai-Mai!" cried Alfie, grabbing her round the knees.

Maia stared. What
was going on? Suddenly
the wardrobe doors
flew open, revealing
an enormous beetle
with red eyes and
sharp pincers.
Rearing up on
its back legs, it
leaped out of the
wardrobe!

CHAPTER NINE

Maia hardly paused to think – she opened herself to the magic current. When she was using her magic she could see where things were going to move a second or two before they did it. But the magic allowed her to see something else, too. There was a glowing outline around the beetle. It wasn't a real beetle. It was just an illusion!

"I don't believe in you!" she said, pointing at it. "You're not real."

The beetle paused.

"You are *not* real!" she repeated firmly.

The beetle vanished in a flash of light.

"Gone!" said Alfie in surprise. "Beetle go poof!"

Maia breathed a sigh of relief. "Yes, beetle go poof!" she said. Crouching down, she pulled Alfie to her and hugged him. "If it comes back, you just have to tell it you don't believe in it. You mustn't be scared – it's not real." She couldn't help wondering why on earth there was a beetle illusion in her little brother's room.

As she pulled Alfie close, something fell out of his trouser pocket. It was the stretchy man

Maia had given him at the fireworks display. Picking it up, she put it on his bookcase next to the bug catcher. "Come on now, put your pyjamas on."

She helped him get changed and took him back downstairs to their mum, then ran to her room and quickly told Bracken everything that had happened.

"I just don't understand," she said. "Why was there a beetle illusion in Alfie's room?"

"It could be a Fear Shade," said Bracken. "They discover people's fears and use illusions to make it seem like those fears are coming to life. The more scared the person gets, the stronger the illusion grows."

"Do you think Fear Shades could be affecting Lottie, Sita and Ionie, too?" Maia said slowly. "Lottie's been really scared about her exam results, Sita's been terrified there's a Shade following her and Ionie…" She paused. "Well, Ionie's been convinced we don't like her but I'm not sure what that has to do with being scared."

"Unless she's scared about not having any friends," said Bracken.

Maia let out a breath. "Of course!" Ionie might often act as if she didn't need anyone at all but she'd been really happy since they'd become friends. Her fear *was* being without friends again. Suddenly she remembered something. "Bracken! In my nightmare the other night, the Shades said, 'We shall make your fears come true!' Well, people's fears *are* coming true – or at least it seems as if they are."

Bracken spun in a circle. "We need to find the objects the Shades are trapped in. What do all your friends have?"

"It has to be something Alfie has, too." Maia shook her head. "I can't think of anything like that…" Then she gasped. "Oh yes, I can! It's the little yellow stretchy men, Bracken! They were attached to the sparkler packets that

Auntie Mabel gave us on bonfire night. I gave my little man to Alfie and the others all kept theirs. But hang on –" she paused, frowning – "Auntie Mabel wouldn't give us something with dark magic in it. Unless…" She started to nod as she made sense of it. "Unless she didn't know. She said she didn't remember the little men being attached to the sparkler packets when she bought them at the shop. Someone must have stuck them on afterwards! It could have been Mrs Crooks even. After all, she only lives next door!"

"We have to get hold of those stretchy men," said Bracken.

"There's one in Alfie's bedroom," said Maia. "Come on, no one's around."

They ran along the landing and into Alfie's room and Maia shut the door. Her eyes fell on the little yellow stretchy man sitting on the bookcase where she had left it.

No. She frowned. She'd left it on the top

shelf and now it was on the second shelf down. Her skin prickled.

"Come here, you!" she whispered, reaching out.

The stretchy man jumped away from her. It scuttled along the shelf and then turned to face her. Its round face became pointed, its hands grew claw-like nails and its face twisted into an evil smile.

With a growl, Bracken leaped at it but it jumped down to the floor. Maia grabbed hold of it but it bit her hard with its sharp teeth.

"Ow!" she gasped, dropping it.

It raced towards the door but Bracken was there in a flash. He leaped in front of it and crouched down, blocking the way. "You're not getting out."

"Oh, I think I am," the stretchy man hissed.

"I'll find someone else whose fears I can make come true." He stretched his hands and his nails grew even longer. "Move, fox, or you'll be sorry!"

"Not as sorry as you'll be for scaring my brother!" Maia grabbed the plastic bug catcher she'd given Alfie and clapped the jaws shut over the stretchy man, trapping him safely inside. "Got you!" she said, holding him up.

"No!" the stretchy man screeched, hammering his little fists against the plastic container.

"Oh yes, and now you and all the other Shades are going back to the shadows where you belong!" Maia picked up a metal tin that Alfie kept cars in. She emptied it and dropped the stretchy man inside, releasing the jaws of the bug catcher and slamming down the lid.

Bracken spun in a circle. "Yay, Maia! You got him!"

Maia grinned. "One caught, just three to go!"

Chapter Ten

Maia persuaded her dad to drive her round to Ionie's by telling him they had some homework they needed to do together. She thought it would be best to go to Ionie's first, then she and Ionie could shadow-travel to Lottie and Sita's houses together. Ionie's mum, Mrs Cooper, answered the door.

"Hello," she said, looking a bit puzzled. "Ionie didn't mention you were coming round this evening."

"Didn't she?" Maia said innocently.

"We arranged it at school."

"Well, come along in. She's in her room."

Maia hurried up the stairs and knocked on Ionie's bedroom door.

"What is it?" Ionie sounded upset.

"Ionie, it's me – Maia."

"Maia?" The door opened. Ionie's cheeks were tear-stained. "What are you doing here?"

Maia shut the door behind her. "Bracken!" she whispered. He appeared in a shimmer. "Call Sorrel," Maia urged Ionie.

Ionie looked confused but did what Maia said. "Sorrel!"

"What's happening?" said the wildcat, as soon as she appeared. Her back arched and she glared at Maia's bag. "Your bag smells of dark magic!"

"I'll tell you more about that in a moment," said Maia. "But first, Ionie—"

"Why are you here?" interrupted Ionie. "You don't like me. You, Sita and Lottie don't want to be friends with me. I bet you all talk about me behind my back. None of you want me to be a Star Friend." Her eyes brimmed with hurt. "You wish I'd never been chosen."

Maia wondered what to do. She'd been able to make the beetle vanish simply by saying she didn't believe in it, but Ionie's fears were all in her head.

"Sorrel's the only friend I've got," said Ionie miserably.

"That's not true!" Maia said. "Ionie, I'm your friend. Please believe me."

Ionie looked at her tearfully.

"It's true," said Bracken, licking her hand. "After you fought the last Shade, Maia told me how glad she was that you were a Star Friend and how pleased she was that you were friends again."

"I think it's a Shade that's making you feel differently," said Maia.

"A Shade?" Ionie echoed.

"Impossible," said Sorrel. "I would know if a Shade had been affecting Ionie."

"You said you'd smelled the traces of a Shade here. Well, it's been moving about," said Bracken. "Probably so that you wouldn't catch it."

"Where is it?" said Sorrel, looking around. "What's it trapped in?"

"Ionie, you know that little yellow stretchy man you got on bonfire night?" Maia said. "The Shade is inside it. There's one in my bag at the moment. We caught it at my house and put it in a tin. It made Alfie think there was a giant beetle in his room."

"They're Fear Shades, I think," Bracken said. "Shades that make people believe their worst fears are coming true."

"Alfie's scared of beetles so he saw a giant beetle," said Maia. "Lottie's biggest fear is failing exams and I think the Shade in her house is making her believe that's going to happen—"

"Sita's really scared of Shades so her Shade has made her believe there's one stalking her," Ionie broke in. "And me … it's been making me think that no one likes me."

"You don't need to be scared of that!" Maia burst out. "We all like you. I mean, I know sometimes you and Lottie don't get on but we all want you to be our friend. We're all glad you're a Star Friend – Lottie as well." She grabbed Ionie's hands. "I promise I'm telling the truth."

As their eyes met, Ionie swallowed. "I

believe you," she said slowly. Her expression gradually cleared. "I've been so stupid!" she exclaimed, pulling away from Maia. "But the feelings I had seemed so real…"

Maia nodded. "The Shade made you believe them."

"Where is this Shade?" hissed Sorrel, her tail fluffing out.

There was a sinister chuckle and a small yellow stretchy man looked out from behind the mirror on Ionie's desk.

"Looks like I've been found out," he said. "And I was having such fun making Ionie think everyone hated her. Tricked you!" He gave a squeaky laugh.

Sorrel sprang on to the desk. The stretchy man somersaulted off and lightly landed on the floor.

"Can't catch me!" he chortled.

He shot across the floor, heading for the slightly open window.

Bracken was after him in a flash, jaws snapping, but the stretchy man zoomed up the wall, using his sticky hands and feet.

He reached for the window ledge and then recoiled with a high-pitched gasp as sharp spikes suddenly shot out of the windowsill.

"What?" he cried. Losing his grip, he tumbled through the air, his limbs waving. As he landed on the floor, Sorrel sprang from the table and caught him in her jaws.

"Let me go!" squawked the stretchy man.

Maia pulled the tin out of her bag, opened the lid and Sorrel spat the man inside. Maia banged the lid back on.

"What just happened?" the little man screeched.

"I think you'll find *I* just tricked *you*!" said

Ionie. "You're not the only one who can cast illusions! I made you see what wasn't there!"

"No!" the little man shrieked, battering at the tin.

"Two down, two to go," said Maia, high-fiving Ionie.

Sorrel gave a smug meow and Bracken bounded over. "Now, that's what I call teamwork!" he said.

"Argh!" Sita squealed, as Ionie and Maia suddenly appeared in the shadows by her wardrobe. She and Willow leaped to the far side of her bedroom and stared at them with wide eyes.

"Ionie? Maia? Is it really you?" Sita cried.

"Yes, we shadow-travelled here together," said Maia, going over to her. She looked at Bracken. "Bracken, guard the door. We'll have to vanish if anyone comes."

"I thought it was the Shade who's been following me!" Sita said. "I—" She broke off with a gasp and pointed to the wardrobe. "The Shade! Look! There it is!"

Hearing a low, sinister laugh, they swung round. A tall figure stepped out of the shadows. Its limbs were angular, its fingers tipped with spiky nails. "Sita, oh, Sita," it hissed.

For a moment, Maia felt her blood freeze. But then she came to her senses. "You're not real!" she said, marching over to it. "I don't believe in you!" And with that, the Shade vanished in a cloud of smoke.

Sita gaped. "What ... what's going on?"

"The Shade was an illusion, Sita. There hasn't really been a Shade following you," said Ionie. "But there has been one affecting you."

"Where's the yellow stretchy man you got on Bonfire Night? The Shade is trapped inside that," said Maia.

"It's in my coat pocket downstairs," said Sita.

"Go and get it," urged Ionie.

Sita hurried out of the room and returned a few moments later with her coat. She pulled the little stretchy man out of the pocket. "There's a Shade inside this?"

"Yes, one who's been making you imagine a Shade was stalking you," said Maia.

As they spoke, the little man started to laugh. Ionie snatched him from Sita before she could drop him. "The tin, Maia! Ow!" she yelped. The stretchy man had grown fangs and it bit Ionie's fingers, but she didn't let go.

Maia pulled out the tin and they stuffed the stretchy man inside with the other two.

"Horrible creature!" said Ionie, shaking her

injured hand.

"Here, I can heal you," said Sita.

She touched Ionie's hand and breathed in deeply. Before their eyes, the wound closed up. Ionie smiled at Sita.

"So, there wasn't really a Shade stalking me, it was just an illusion?" Sita said.

"Yes, caused by that Shade," said Maia. "I think that Mrs Crooks has somehow worked out we're Star Friends and that she stuck those stretchy men to the sparklers before Auntie Mabel gave them to us."

"But why?" said Sita.

"To distract us from following her!"

Sita frowned. "But she'd only just met us earlier that day."

"Well," said Maia, realizing that Sita was right, "maybe she knew we were Star Friends before she actually met us. That could be why she was so horrible to us in the clearing."

"OK, but if she was putting Shades into

the stretchy men, why does she have all those gnomes?" Sita said.

Maia frowned. She couldn't think of an answer to that.

"Right now we haven't got time to figure this out," said Ionie. "We have to help Lottie." She held out her hands. "Come on, let's shadow-travel!"

When they arrived in Lottie's room, everything was neat and tidy, like always, but Lottie was sitting on the floor with a letter in her hands, in tears. Juniper was stroking her hair with his little paws. "Don't cry, please don't cry," he was begging.

"But I've failed my piano exam." Lottie picked up another letter from the floor beside her. "And the maths challenge."

"Hi, Lottie!" Maia said.

Lottie almost jumped out of her skin.

The girls called their animals' names and they appeared, too.

Lottie stared. "Why are you all here? What's going on?" she whispered.

"Well, it's like this—" Ionie began.

"Shh!" Lottie said hastily. "Mum and Dad are downstairs!"

"We'll be quiet," promised Maia in a quiet voice.

"Well, we'll try," said Sita, looking around anxiously.

"So why did you come?" demanded Lottie. "Was it because you heard about my exam results?" She held up the letters. "I failed maths and piano."

"I don't think you did." Maia really hoped she was right. She let magic tingle through her. To her relief, the letters in Lottie's hand started to glow with a shining outline. "They're just an illusion!" She touched them. "You're not real," she said.

When the letters vanished, Lottie gasped.
"What happened?"

"A Fear Shade made those letters appear,"
Maia explained. "It made you believe your
fears were coming true. You haven't failed
your exams."

Lottie stared. "Really? Oh my goodness,
I've been so worried. So it was all a Shade?"

The others nodded.

There was a slight rustling noise and
Bracken and Sorrel swung round to see a
stretchy man creeping across Lottie's desk.

"There it is!" said Bracken.

The stretchy man started to run but in a flash, Juniper had jumped on to the table and grabbed him in his paws. "You're going nowhere!" Juniper exclaimed.

"Apart from back to the shadows!" added Ionie.

The stretchy man struggled in Juniper's grasp.

Maia took the box out of her bag and opened it just enough to get the little man in and then slammed it shut. "Got him!" She looked at the others. "Now what do we do?"

"We need to send them back to the shadows," said Lottie.

"How exactly do you plan to do that?" said Sorrel. "Do I have to remind you that Ionie must be looking a Shade in the eyes to be able to command it? That may be a problem."

Maia bit her lip. Sorrel was right. The stretchy men moved so fast when they were free – and there were four of them. How could Ionie hope to be able to look them all in the eye at the same time?

"Perhaps we should try sending them back one at a time," said Lottie. "If we open the tin and take one out, Ionie could try and command it."

The lid on the tin shifted upwards slightly as the stretchy men inside tried to get out.

"We'd better be quick!" said Sita. "This could go horribly wrong if they all escape."

"OK, let's open the lid," said Lottie. "Ionie, get ready."

"Remember, they bite," warned Maia. "Here goes!" She loosened one corner of the lid of the tin.

WHAM! The lid exploded off the tin and the stretchy men leaped out.

Sita screamed and Maia ducked as one jumped over her shoulder. Ionie staggered back as another launched itself straight at her face with its claws out. Luckily Lottie saw what was happening and, using her super-speed, she sprang in front of Ionie and batted it away just in time. It flew through the air and landed on the floor.

"Thank you!" Ionie gasped.

The animals sprang into action, trying to pounce and grab but the stretchy men seemed to be everywhere. One of them reached the door and Maia realized the man was planning on squeezing underneath it.

"Stop it!" she cried.

Maia and Ionie both threw themselves forwards but even as Maia felt her fingers close round it, it seemed to slip out from between her fingers.

"It's escaping!" cried Ionie.

"Freeze! Everyone, freeze!" exclaimed Sita.

All of a sudden Maia found she couldn't move. What was going on? She could see that everyone – her friends, the animals and even the stretchy men – were frozen to the spot.

"Oh," Sita said faintly, looking around the room. "I didn't think it would work that well."

Maia's thoughts raced. How had Sita made everyone do as she said?

Sita took a trembling breath. "OK, listen to me. Maia, Lottie and Ionie, I want you all to unfreeze. Bracken, Willow, Juniper and Sorrel, too. *Unfreeze!*"

It was as if a magic wand had been waved. Suddenly Maia found she could move again.

"What's going on?" Lottie said, staring at Sita, who was standing in the middle of the room looking rather sheepish.

Willow trotted over to Sita. "Your magic, Sita," she said softly. "It's just as we thought."

"I know," said Sita in a small voice. "I'm not sure I like it." Willow nuzzled her.

"What are you talking about?" demanded Ionie.

"Yes, enough of talking in riddles. Will one of you please explain what just happened?" said Sorrel sharply.

Sita put her hand on Willow's head. "Um … we were planning to tell you all about it but then everything started going wrong and I couldn't focus on anything other than the Shade I thought was stalking me. You know we all thought my magic was to do with healing and soothing people?"

They all nodded.

"Well, it *is* about healing but I think that the soothing part isn't quite what it seems. People do calm down when I tell them to…" She glanced at Willow for help.

"But it's because Sita's magic lets her command others," explained Willow. "If she tells them to do something, they have to do it. People, animals, Shades."

Maia looked round at the four little stretchy men still frozen in position – one halfway under the door, one crouching down, one bending over, one on his tummy. Their eyes were rolling furiously as they fought against the magic but they couldn't move.

"That's awesome," breathed Lottie.

"And scary," said Sita, with a slight shake to her voice.

"Sita, you must be the really powerful one the Shade told us about!" Maia realized.

"But I don't want to be," Sita said.

"I don't think you have a choice," said Bracken.

Sorrel gazed at Sita. "You will be in danger. A person using dark magic would do anything for your kind of power."

"Oh," Sita whispered.

Lottie picked up a frozen stretchy man that was lying near to her. "Look, let's talk about this more after we've sent these Shades back to the shadows." She looked at Willow. "Can Sita do that?"

"No, Sita can command them in this world but only a Spirit Speaker like Ionie can send spirits between worlds," Willow said.

"But what Sita can do is command the Shades to look Ionie in the eyes," said Sorrel.

She picked up a stretchy man in her mouth and held it up to Ionie.

Lottie nudged Sita. "Go on then. Do your commanding thing."

"Stretchy men, I … um … want you all to look at Ionie," said Sita.

Sure enough, all four stretchy men reluctantly looked at Ionie.

"Go back to the shadows where you

belong!" Ionie said. The Shades shivered and shook and then, with a last wide-eyed look, they fell still.

"It worked!" said Sita in delight.

The animals bounded around the room.

"Well done, Sita," said Willow.

"That was brilliant!" yapped Bracken.

"Shh!" said Lottie, glancing towards the door.

"You did exceptionally well," Sorrel purred to Ionie.

"The Shades have really gone," Ionie said in a low voice. "It's over!"

Maia shook her head. "No, it's not."

"What do you mean?" said Ionie.

Maia took a deep breath. "We've still got Mrs Crooks to deal with."

CHAPTER ELEVEN

Ionie grabbed Maia's hand. "Time to shadow-travel to Mrs Crooks's house!"

"No," said Sita quickly. "Not now. It's late. Imagine what will happen if our parents come looking for us and we're not in our bedrooms? They might even have discovered we're missing already."

Maia hesitated but Sita was right. "OK, we'll go round to her house tomorrow after school then."

The others all nodded.

They said goodbye to Lottie and all their Star Animals and then Ionie shadow-travelled with Sita and Maia back to Sita's house. Leaving Sita there they went on to Ionie's. As they arrived in the shadows beside her wardrobe, there was a knock on her bedroom door.

"Do you two need anything?" Ionie's mum said, opening the door and looking in. "How's the homework going?"

"Fine. We've just finished, Mum," said Ionie, smoothing down her hair.

Maia nodded. "I'll call my dad and ask him to collect me."

"Don't worry, I can drop you home," Ionie's mum said.

Maia and Ionie shared a look of relief – that had been close. What would have happened it they hadn't got back in time? Shadow-travel was amazing but very risky.

As Mrs Cooper drove Maia and Ionie past

Mrs Crooks's cottage on the way back to her house, Maia wondered what Mrs Crooks was doing. All the lights were off in the cottage. Was she out in the woods gathering plants and herbs to do more dark magic? Maia shivered. How could they possibly stop her?

Sita, Maia realized, thinking of Sita's new power. She'd be able to command Mrs Crooks. *Tomorrow,* Maia thought. *Tomorrow we'll stop the dark magic once and for all.*

✦ ✦ ✦

After school the next day, the girls asked if they could go for a walk and then have tea at Maia's house. To their relief, all their parents agreed. They headed to Mrs Crooks's cottage and stopped on the street. "OK," said Ionie. "As soon as she opens the door, you've got to use your magic, Sita, and make her ask us in. Then, once we're in, you need to command her to tell us about the dark magic she's been doing."

"I'm scared," said Sita, her eyes wide.

Maia squeezed her hand. "Don't be. We'll all be with you."

They started to walk down the drive but, before they could reach the door, Mrs Crooks came out. "What are you girls doing here?" she demanded.

Her dog ran out and started barking at them. It snapped at Sita's ankles, making her squeal and back away.

"Jack! Stop that! Come here!" called Mrs Crooks. "You girls, clear off!" she said angrily. "You heard me, go away! Stop upsetting my dog!"

With all the noise and confusion, Sita didn't have a chance to try and use her magic on Mrs Crooks.

"We're not upsetting him!" Ionie shouted.

"Whatever's going on here?" Hearing a familiar voice, Maia swung round and saw Mary from the Copper Kettle tea shop. "Jenny,

what's happening? Jack, come here! Stop
making all that noise."

To Maia's surprise, the dog stopped barking
and ran over to Mary, greeting her with a
wagging tail. Mary took hold of his collar.

"These children are bothering him, Mary,"
said Mrs Crooks angrily. "Hanging around on
my drive. Trying to upset him."

Mary shook her head. "These girls are lovely.
They wouldn't do that – they all adore animals."

Mrs Crooks harrumphed.

"Girls, I'm sorry about this. Please excuse my sister," Mary said to them. "She's not very keen on young people, you see."

Maia stared. Mary and horrible Mrs Crooks were sisters? Yes, now she looked, she could see similarities between them but Mary's face was open and smiling whereas Mrs Crooks's was closed and suspicious.

"Calm down, Jenny. I promise you, these girls wouldn't ever hurt an animal. Would you, girls?" Mary went on.

"Never, we all love animals," said Ionie.

"We really do," Lottie said, holding her hand out to the dog. He growled.

"Sorry, Lottie," Mary said. "Jack's not very good with young people. He was a stray who was badly treated by some teenagers once. That's why he's only got one ear. He came into the vet's where Jenny used to work. She helped get him better and then adopted him."

"Oh," Maia said slowly.

"Jenny's working at the new wildlife sanctuary," Mary went on.

Maia's mind spun as she tried to match Mrs Crooks the conjurer of Shades with Mrs Crooks the animal lover that Mary was telling her about.

"We've got badgers and foxes and rabbits and hedgehogs," said Mrs Crooks, slightly gruffly. "Polecats, squirrels and weasels. Some of the animals we keep away from visitors – those who aren't too badly injured and who are going to be released back into the wild. The ones that need a lot of care become too trusting of people, so they have to stay at the sanctuary. They're often injured because of young people –" she fixed them with a look –"leaving litter in the woods. But Mary's right, if you like wildlife you should come and visit."

Mary smiled. "Maybe today they could have a quick look in your shed, Jenny?"

Shed! Maia saw the others' eyes all widen.

Mrs Crooks nodded. "I don't see why not. Provided you're quiet and don't touch anything,"

"What's in the shed?" Ionie ventured.

A rare smile lifted the corners of Mrs Crooks's mouth. "Animals," she said. "Would you like to see?"

The girls exchanged looks. For a moment, Maia wondered if Mary and Mrs Crooks were doing dark magic together. She wanted to see inside the shed – after all it was what they had come here for – but was it an elaborate trap?

"Um … our parents probably wouldn't like us to come in without getting permission first," Lottie said slowly.

"Of course," said Mary. "Good girls, that's very sensible of you."

Just then a car pulled up. "Hi, girls," said Mrs Greene, putting down the window. "Is everything OK?"

"Everything's fine," said Mary.

"Mum –" Maia felt a bit nervous but she knew she had to get to the bottom of this – "Mrs Crooks has just asked us if we want to see inside her shed. Is it OK if we do?"

"Jenny's got some animals in there," said Mary.

"Sure," said Mrs Greene. "I'm just popping to the shop to get some cheese and ham. I can pick you up on the way back. Dad's made some pizza dough so you can make your own pizzas for tea."

The girls nodded and followed Mrs Crooks into the house. There were pictures of animals on the walls and the kitchen smelled of baking bread.

"Come through this way," said Mrs Crooks.

As the girls stepped through the back door into the garden they all gasped. There were pottery gnomes everywhere! They all had jolly faces – some were fishing in a pond, others pushing wheelbarrows or carrying baskets.

There were also pottery toadstools and
animals. "Oh ... wow!" said Maia.

"I collect garden ornaments," Mrs Crooks
said, looking pleased at their reaction.

Mary smiled. "Do you like them, girls?"

"Yes," said Maia, looking around in
astonishment. Sorrel had been right, there were
lots of gnomes ... but they weren't sinister.
The garden was like a fairy tale woodland
scene.

"I'd love a garden like this," said Sita.

"Jenny's been collecting since we were
children," said Mary. "Some of them are really

valuable now."

"Is that why you have such a high fence?"
Lottie asked.

Mrs Crooks nodded. "I had a couple of
pieces stolen from the garden at my old house
so I had the fence put up when I moved in
here." She headed up a winding gravel path.
Reaching the shed, she put her finger to her
lips and opened the door. It was dark inside
and the air was filled with the scent of hay and
animals. There were cages just as Maia had seen
in her mirror. Some were empty but others had
animals in – the girls could see that some of
them had bandages or wounds that had been
recently stitched up. The animals blinked warily
at the girls in the dim light.

"There's a squirrel," whispered Lottie.

"And rabbits and a baby badger," murmured
Ionie.

"These animals will all be released into the
wild again soon," Mrs Crooks said in a low

voice. "When I find an injured animal I bring them here first. The vet comes to assess them and takes the ones that need a lot of veterinary help to the sanctuary." Her face softened as she looked at them. "They're my little beauties and I try my best to help them so they can be set free."

Maia swallowed. She suddenly realized that they'd been so, so wrong about Mrs Crooks. She wasn't the person doing dark magic. She was just an old woman who loved animals.

"Jenny goes out into the woods looking for injured animals," said Mary.

"I'm sorry if I've been bad-tempered with you, girls," Mrs Crooks said gruffly. "So many young people don't think about how their actions affect the wildlife – they leave litter, set off fireworks that scare animals, disturb their nests and habitats."

"We'd never do that," Sita said.

"I realize that now," said Mrs Crooks. "I'm

sorry. I shouldn't have been so quick to judge."

She pulled the door shut and the girls followed her back up the garden path. As Maia saw the gnomes again, she thought of something. "Mrs Crooks, did you give a gnome to the Eastons?"

"The Eastons? No, I don't know who you mean," said Mrs Crooks.

"They live on Brook Street. There's a big trampoline in the front garden," said Maia, feeling puzzled. She'd definitely seen Mrs Crooks with the Wish Gnome – so either the magic had been wrong or Mrs Crooks was lying.

Mrs Crooks's face cleared. "Oh, I know that house. They do have a gnome in the garden, don't they? I picked it up to look at it a week or so ago when I was passing. I couldn't resist. It was a nice specimen, and yes, just like some of mine, but no, I didn't give it to them."

Maia's breath left her in a rush. So the image she'd seen had been Mrs Crooks admiring the gnome, but she hadn't been the person who had given it to Paige's mum. "Thank you for showing us the animals," she said.

"Yes, and we'll come and visit the sanctuary soon," said Sita.

"Make sure you come and find me when you do," said Mrs Crooks, leading them through the house and letting them out of the front door. "And I'll give you a guided tour."

They said goodbye and she shut the door.

The girls looked at each other. "OK, so maybe we got it wrong," said Lottie slowly.

They all nodded. "We really did," said Maia.

"But if Mrs Crooks didn't conjure the Shades, who did?" said Sita.

"I still think it must be someone who knows we're Star Friends," said Ionie.

Maia lifted her chin. "Well, they can try all they like but they're not going to stop us – we're going to find out who's using dark magic."

"They've got no chance against us," Lottie

said. "Not with Sita's power."

"It's *all* of our powers that will stop them," said Sita.

Lottie smiled. "The important thing is that we did it – we sent all four Shades back to the shadows."

"And next we'll deal with whoever it is using dark magic," said Maia. "Won't we?" She held her up hand.

"Definitely," they all chorused, high-fiving her.

Just then there was a pip of a car horn and Mrs Greene pulled up alongside them. "Ready for some homemade pizza, girls?" she asked, and the friends all piled into the car.

Maia looked out of the window at the pretty village of Westcombe as they drove back to her house. Together with her friends and their Star Animals, they would keep everyone safe and happy. Nothing and no one was going to stop them.

About the Author

Linda Chapman is the best-selling author of over 200 books. The biggest compliment Linda can have is for a child to tell her they became a reader after reading one of her books. Linda lives in a cottage with a tower in Leicestershire with her husband, three children, three dogs and three ponies. When she's not writing, Linda likes to ride, read and visit schools and libraries to talk to people about writing.

www.lindachapmanauthor.co.uk

About the Illustrator

Lucy Fleming has been an avid doodler and bookworm since early childhood. Drawing always seemed like so much fun but she never dreamed it could be a full-time job! She lives and works in a small town in England with her partner and a little black cat. When not at her desk she likes nothing more than to be outdoors in the sunshine with a hot cup of tea.

www.lucyflemingillustrations.com